Beep, Beep!

W9-BQX-303

Written by
Barbara Gregorich

Illustrated by
Ed Taber

Beep, beep!

Beep, beep!

Look at all the sheep!

Beep, beep!

They can't take long.

I'll sing a song.

They will take all day!

I'll back away.

They will make me late!

I'll close the gate.

Oh, no!

Beep, beep!

Help!
There are too many sheep!

I give up. I'll go to sleep.

He went to sleep
and so did the sheep.